- LOOK AND FIND -

GARGOYLES

Illustrated by Jaime Diaz Studios

Written by Gary Louis

Lettered by Kelly Hume

Published by
Louis Weber, C.E.O.
Publications International, Ltd.
7373 North Cicero Avenue
Lincolnwood, Illinois 60646

Manufactured in U.S.A.

8 7 6 5 4 3 2 1

ISBN 0-7853-1351-6

PUBLICATIONS INTERNATIONAL, LTD.

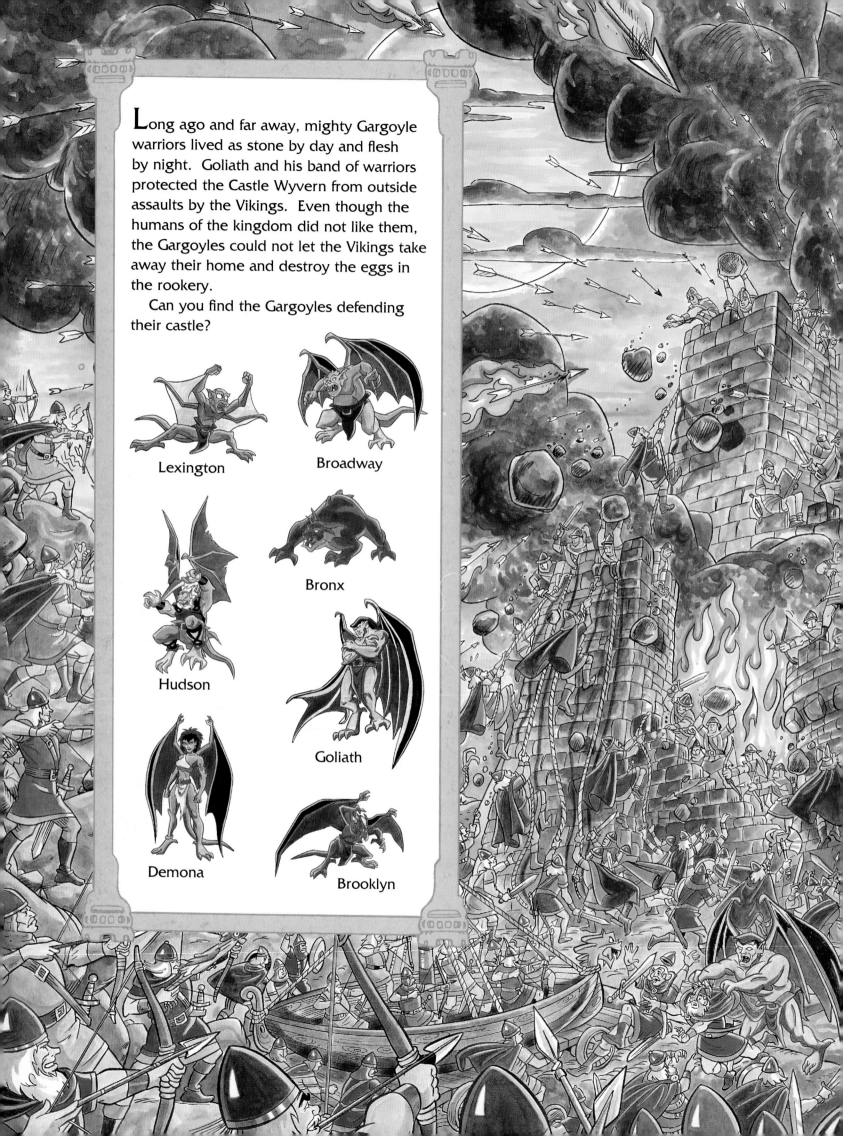

Long ago and far away, mighty Gargoyle warriors lived as stone by day and flesh by night. Goliath and his band of warriors protected the Castle Wyvern from outside assaults by the Vikings. Even though the humans of the kingdom did not like them, the Gargoyles could not let the Vikings take away their home and destroy the eggs in the rookery.

Can you find the Gargoyles defending their castle?

Lexington

Broadway

Bronx

Hudson

Goliath

Demona

Brooklyn

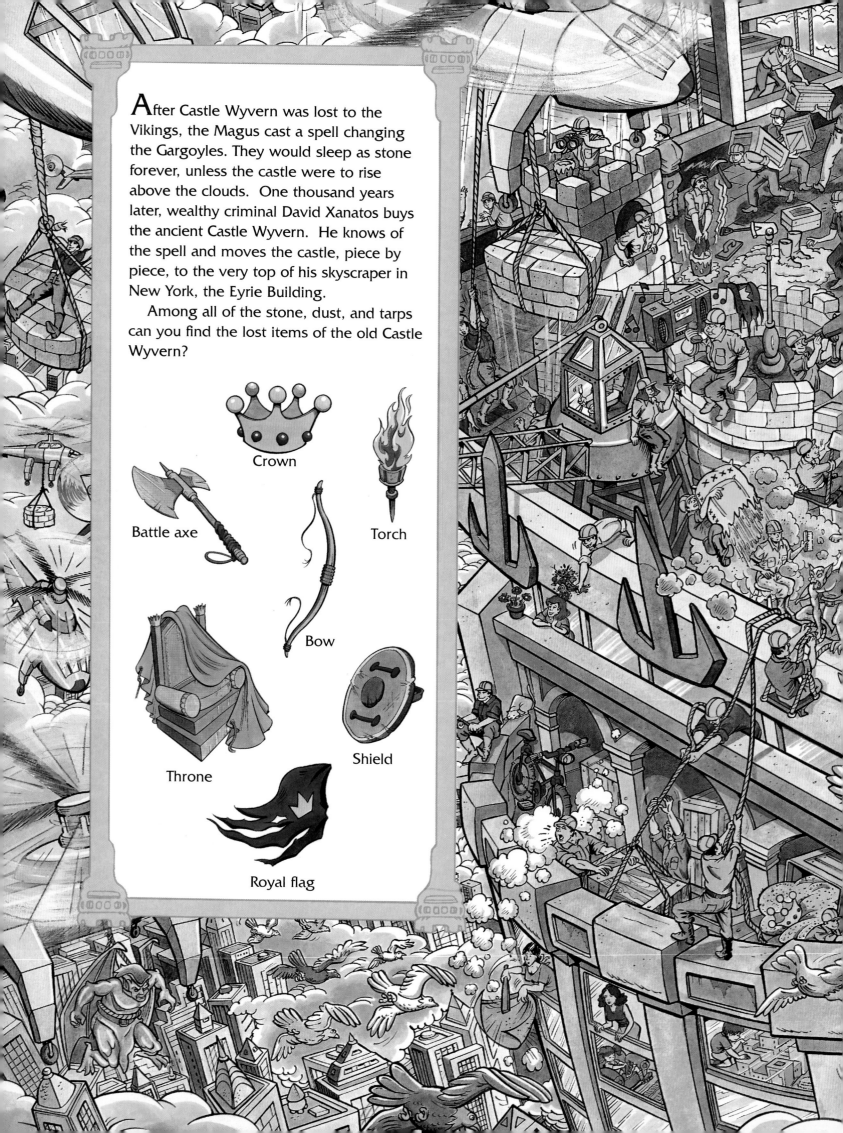

After Castle Wyvern was lost to the Vikings, the Magus cast a spell changing the Gargoyles. They would sleep as stone forever, unless the castle were to rise above the clouds. One thousand years later, wealthy criminal David Xanatos buys the ancient Castle Wyvern. He knows of the spell and moves the castle, piece by piece, to the very top of his skyscraper in New York, the Eyrie Building.

Among all of the stone, dust, and tarps can you find the lost items of the old Castle Wyvern?

Crown

Battle axe

Torch

Bow

Throne

Shield

Royal flag

When the Gargoyles' move to the top of the Eyrie Building is complete, the sun goes down and the Gargoyles awake from their thousand-year sleep. They awake just as a group of Cyberbiotic intruders looking for top-secret computer disks attacks the castle. The Gargoyles need your help to defeat the trespassers.

Help find and destroy the weapons and supplies that the Cyberbiotic intruders use to attack the castle. Then find the disks before the intruders find them.

Sledgehammer

These disks

Dynamite

Crossbow

Night vision glasses

Walkie-talkie

Tear gas canister

Utility knife

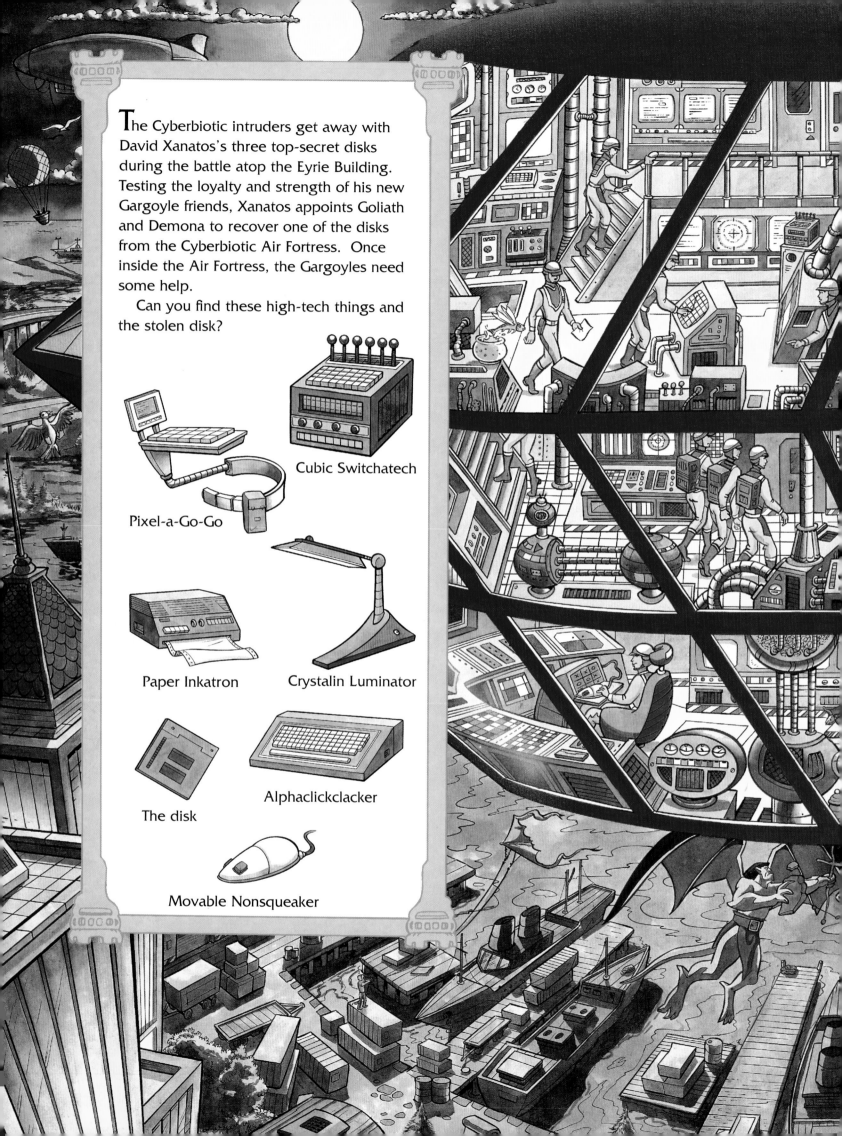

The Cyberbiotic intruders get away with David Xanatos's three top-secret disks during the battle atop the Eyrie Building. Testing the loyalty and strength of his new Gargoyle friends, Xanatos appoints Goliath and Demona to recover one of the disks from the Cyberbiotic Air Fortress. Once inside the Air Fortress, the Gargoyles need some help.

Can you find these high-tech things and the stolen disk?

Cubic Switchatech

Pixel-a-Go-Go

Paper Inkatron

Crystalin Luminator

The disk

Alphaclickclacker

Movable Nonsqueaker

Not knowing who to trust in this strange new world, the winged warriors must learn about modern-day society any way they can. The television provides information and entertainment to Brooklyn, Lexington, and Broadway, whose favorite program is *The Pack.* When the members of The Pack appear live at Madison Square Garden, the Gargoyles make sure that they get front-rafter seats.

See if you can spot the young Gargoyles among the fans. Find the members of The Pack doing what they do best.

Wolf

Dingo

Fox

Jackal

Hyena

After seeing humans riding motorcycles one night, Lexington decides to rebuild an old motorcycle for Brooklyn. While riding, Brooklyn comes upon an unfriendly gang on their motorcycles. The motorcycle gang realizes that Brooklyn is not a human, and they want to fight with him.

Help Brooklyn by locating the other Gargoyles and their new friend, Elisa Maza.

Goliath

Lexington

Hudson

Elisa Maza

Bronx

Demona

Broadway

The Gargoyles have discovered that David Xanatos is an evil man. They uncovered his plan to smuggle stolen museum jewels inside stone statues. The statues, made by Xanatos's artist friend, are meant to look like collectors' pieces. The Gargoyles are trying to find the stolen jewels hidden inside the smuggler's art studio to return them to their proper owners.

Help the Gargoyles stop Xanatos's illegal scheme by finding the stolen jewels.

Pearl necklace

Golden candlesticks

Jewel-covered shoes

Gem-covered goblet

Crown of jewels

Diamond ring

Diamond bracelet

Diamond-hilted Excalibur

EXANATOS UNUM

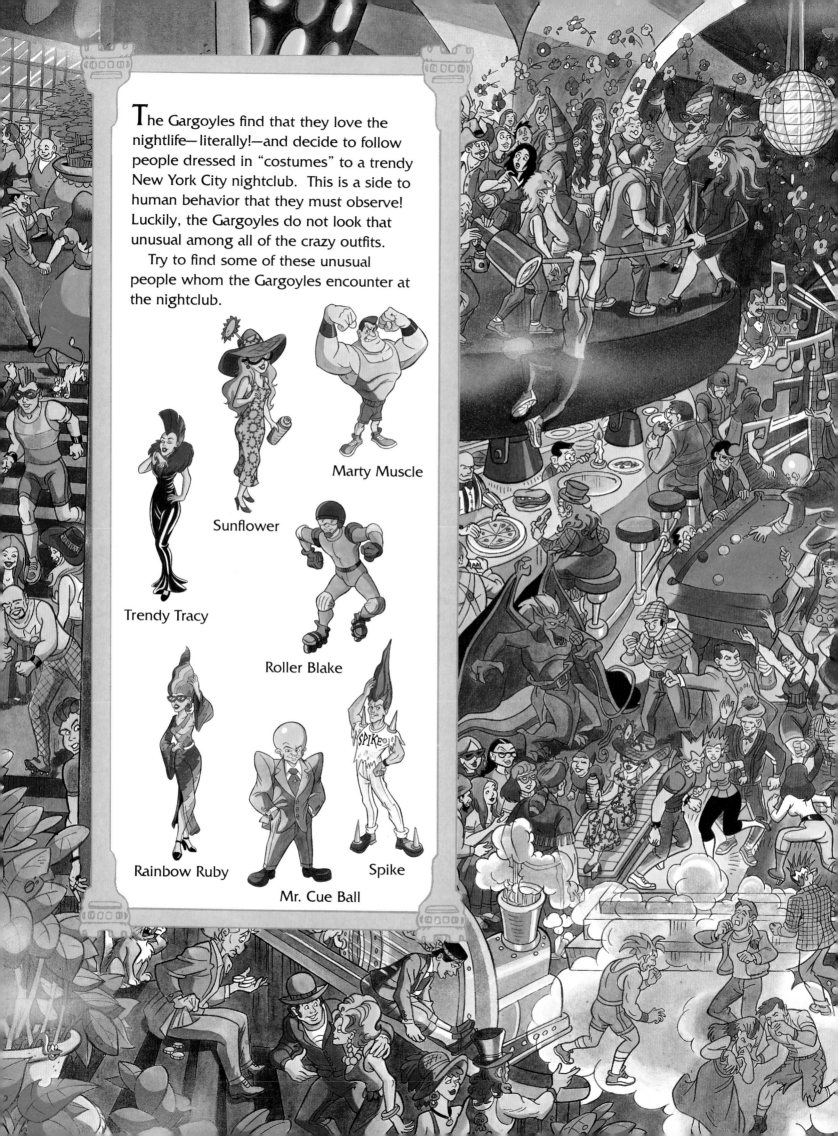

The Gargoyles find that they love the nightlife—literally!—and decide to follow people dressed in "costumes" to a trendy New York City nightclub. This is a side to human behavior that they must observe! Luckily, the Gargoyles do not look that unusual among all of the crazy outfits.

Try to find some of these unusual people whom the Gargoyles encounter at the nightclub.

Sunflower

Marty Muscle

Trendy Tracy

Roller Blake

Rainbow Ruby

Mr. Cue Ball

Spike

Modern society holds many dangers for the Gargoyles, but also offers many fun activities. Video games are one source of entertainment that makes the Gargoyles "crack" a smile. They've even found an incredibly huge video arcade not far from their home. Everyone at the arcade has so much fun playing the games, no one seems to notice the strange "oversized kids."

Look around and see the things that make this arcade entertaining for such stoney characters.

Popcorn

Cotton candy

A clown

Game token

Balloons

A jukebox

Prize teddy bear

Wonder Pony